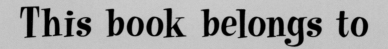

This book belongs to

....

But guess what happens when
My sister pulls my hair?
Then I turn **RED**.
I'm as angry as a bear!

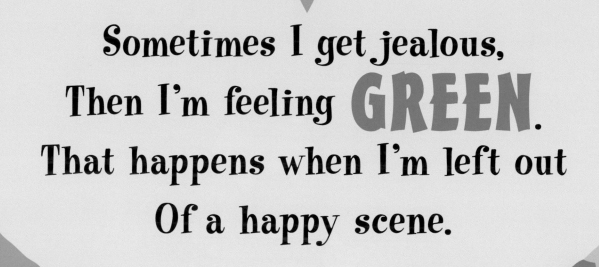

Sometimes I get jealous,
Then I'm feeling **GREEN**.
That happens when I'm left out
Of a happy scene.

When I'm feeling scared,
Kids call me YELLOW,
But I can find my courage
And be a brave fellow!

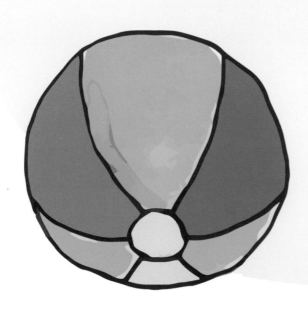